ONE LAST TIME

ANDINO + HAVEN
BOOK 3

A COMPANION

BETHANY-KRIS

Published by Bethany-Kris
www.bethanykris.com

ISBN 13: 978-1-989658-13-0

Editor: Eli Peters

Proofreaders: Eli, Tracy, Felicia, Mia.

Cover Design © Mignon Mykel

For every reader that wanted to see these two lovers one last time …

CONTENTS

ONE

"You've passed that same building four times now," Alex said to Andino's left in the backseat of the black Rolls-Royce.

Here we go again, Andino thought.

From the front of the car, where the man did his best work driving only, Nate muttered, "I was told to drive in circles, asshole."

"Does it have to be *actual* circles, though?"

Good God.

These men were going to have Andino on fucking nerve pills before the end of the year—he was sure of it.

"He's fine," Andino said, joining the conversation to end the bickering between the enforcer and the man who now acted as his underboss. "Back to what you were doing—both of you."

1

Thankfully, the men did just that.

Mostly.

If he let them get started now, they wouldn't shut up for the rest of the day. It was one of the things he missed most about having Pink—who had went over to John's side of things as the man's underboss a while back—work for him, if he were being honest. The man knew when to shut up and not engage. These two didn't understand either of those things but especially not with one another.

Andino figured the constant bumping of heads was probably a good sign the two liked each other. On another day, he might have even gotten a chuckle out of it just because. Not today, however. He was tired, annoyed, and wanted to be anywhere, doing anything other than what he currently was.

Business was odd sometimes.

La famiglia worked in funny ways.

Like how right now, he was stuck in the back of a car waiting for a phone call to confirm a meeting that he hadn't even wanted to have was good to go, and

Andino's driver could pull into the business just two blocks over where it was meant to happen. He would much rather be at home with his wife and three daughters, but after eight years of being the Marcello Don, he had come to learn bosses didn't get days off in the mafia.

Something had to happen.

A boss was always needed.

It didn't help that the very last thing Andino liked to do on any given day was wake up earlier than he needed to just to travel into the city, and then drive around aimlessly while someone else decided whether or not to sit down with him. That wasn't how this was supposed to work, and he especially hated it when someone wasted his motherfucking time.

Yet, he was also slightly more forgiving than the boss that came before him, if only because he understood how life could get in the way of business at times. So, instead of immediately calling off the day and the meeting that *should* happen, he put his attention on his phone and texted back and forth with his wife while he waited.

3

It was the best he could do.

For now.

The meeting at the club went fine, read his wife's last text.

Andino smiled to himself and replied back with a simple, *Great, babe.*

He knew better than to ask or say anything more about her club. She'd taken possession of the business the year after they married. Haven essentially—with little fanfare—assured her husband that if he tried anything funny with this club like he did her first one, that she would quickly remove his testicles. He happened to like those right where they were. She was also a damn good business owner, and he understood she didn't need him sticking his nose into her business anyway.

So, he stayed far away.

Happy wife, happy life.

He had this shit on lock.

Her next text came in just as quickly with a question: *How's your meeting going?*

He sighed, wondering how to reply to that. She never outright asked about his business, but she liked to be informed just enough to feel safe. Usually, he would indulge her because he didn't have a reason not to. With this particular day, he didn't think it was quite the same considering it seemed to be going to shit anyway. What did it matter if she knew that? It was just yet another thing for his wife to stress over.

Completely unnecessary.

Fine, he decided to reply.

Really, his wife typed back, *because your little dot on my app keeps circling the same block.*

Damn.

Yeah, he'd forgotten about that. It was actually him who downloaded that app on his wife's phone. He had the same one on his own, too. Their oldest daughter—Lynn—who was seven and had a cell phone with preprogrammed numbers that she could call also had one. His other two girls—Rose was six and Emily Cecelia had just turned four about two weeks prior—wore stylish watches that allowed their parents to check on their location using the same app.

It wasn't that he thought something might happen, but he would rather be prepared if it did.

That's all.

Business as usual, he settled on typing back to Haven. He waited on a reply from her, but didn't get anything right away.

"Yeah, *ciao*, Alex here," the man to Andino's right said.

For a moment, he lifted his attention away from his own phone. It allowed him to see the way Alex's gaze narrowed as he listened to whatever was said on the other end of his call.

"*Really*? No, that won't be happening now. Let him know."

Without another word, his underboss hung up the phone and made a harsh noise before stuffing the device into his pocket.

"What?" Andino asked.

"Your potential associate—"

"He's not a potential associate."

Andino knew that already. Better everyone else did, too. He was simply indulging this bullshit.

Alex cleared his throat, correcting himself with, "Right. *Mr. Moshka* sent someone in his place to do the meeting."

Yeah. No.

Bosses didn't meet with subordinates.

"He's not to get another chance at a meeting with me," Andino said. "Make sure they all know it, Alex."

"Will do."

To his driver, Andino said, "Nate, take me home."

"Sure, boss."

TWO

Haven pulled her large SUV into the drive of her mother-in-law's suburban home just outside the city limits, and parked the vehicle. Looking over the front of the house, a smile curved her lips as she had no doubt her daughters were having the time of their life with their Nana Kim. The house was likely loud and lively at the moment. There was nothing Kim loved more than her grandchildren, truly.

A lot of the time, Andino's mother looked after the three girls when they were out of school, and Haven needed a sitter because of work conflicts. Not that she had much of a problem with that—being the owner of a business and the boss meant she could make whatever schedule she needed to suit her own needs, even though she tried not to take advantage of it.

Today was one of those days that just couldn't be helped. She needed to have a meeting at the club and more people tended to show up when it happened later in the afternoon once they had all gotten in a decent sleep after a late night. Kim had been quick to take the girls—with a smile and all.

She never said no.

Haven was lucky that way.

The phone she'd tossed on the passenger seat after leaving the club flashed with an unanswered text that had come in while she was driving. Reaching over to grab her purse and the phone, she straightened in the seat and checked the phone.

I'm heading home, Andino had wrote. *See you there, babe. Ti amo.*

Haven smiled but didn't bother to reply. She would see him soon enough—once she got all three of their daughters piled into the SUV and took off, that was. Despite the fact he'd sent the text almost a half an hour ago, she would still arrive home before he did, likely.

City driving sucked.

Bad.

Shoving the phone into her purse, Haven exited the SUV and headed for the front stoop of the house. She didn't bother to knock on her in-law's door. The last time she did that—*years ago*—Kim made sure she understood just fine that they were welcome anytime, and the door was always unlocked. Haven still thought she should probably knock, but hey, it wasn't her house.

She hadn't been wrong, either.

The house was loud *and* lively. She barely caught sight of her youngest darting between the doorways in the entry hallway before the girl was out of sight completely. Following behind her was Kim, who laughed just as loud as the girls.

Nothing unusual to see here.

Then, when her oldest daughter came out of the living room with a tablet in hand, Lynn just happened to see her mom standing at the front door. Smiling wide, the girl—all of seven—reminded Haven *so much* of her younger self. Yet, the girl took a lot from her father, too. Like Andino's dark hair, the shape of his lips, and even the color of his eyes.

"Hey, Ma!" Lynn called excitedly.

Haven barely managed to drop her purse before her kid had come down the hallway to greet her with arms thrown wide. She caught Lynn in a hug that she hoped voiced just how much she missed her oldest when she was away from her for a whole day. Before long, her other two girls came around the corner to say hello to their mom, too.

Hugs and kisses galore.

She loved all of it.

Haven wore many hats—some days, she got to be just herself; a tattooed woman in her thirties who liked to keep crazy colors in her hair and ran a strip club in the evenings. Other times, she had to put all of that aside to be the woman that stood beside her crime boss husband. She was a friend, a daughter, and *more*.

Her favorite hat to wear, however, was *mom*.

"Missed you, Ma," her youngest, Emily Cecelia, said in her little girl voice that had not entirely cleared of a childish babble. It always made her smile. "I *wuv* you."

Haven grinned. "I love you, too. Did you have fun with Nana?"

"Well," came a familiar voice from down the hall, "Giovanni just fell asleep upstairs about ten minutes before you came, if that tells you anything about how our day here went."

Laughing, Haven stood to greet her mother-in-law. She shared a hug with Kim while the girls continued to mill about around them. Rose, her middle child, didn't let go of her legs, though.

"They played him out, did they?" she asked.

Kim shrugged. "Gio still thinks he can do all that he used to do—we don't point out that he can't, you know."

Ah.

Yeah.

"Thanks again for looking after them today—I know they're a handful."

Kim shrugged and smiled fondly at her granddaughters who—without even needing to be told—were already pulling on their jackets and shoes. Or rather, Lynn was helping Emily, and Rose was putting her shoes on the wrong feet.

Kids.

It was a work in progress.

Haven loved it, though.

"Oh, I'll never complain about getting them. Not after I spent years hounding Andino for grandbabies."

Yes, her greatest wish.

Then, Kim gave Haven a look. She could tell her mother-in-law was carefully choosing her words when she asked, "Did you hear anything about your next round?"

Just like that, Haven's mood dipped a little. She was mindful not to show it. All of them were extra cautious not to put adult problems on her girls, but sometimes, they slipped up. Not lately, thankfully.

"The office called today," Haven replied. "We'll be going in soon for it."

"Oh, that's good, then. Is this the last one?"

That made Haven sigh.

"It is."

Their last round of IVF.

Their last chance at one more baby.

Before this, it had seemed like all Haven needed to do was jump in bed with Andino and somehow, they'd end up pregnant again. And then a couple of years passed after Emily Cecelia's birth where *nothing* happened. They tried for a while on their own before going for a specialist consultation.

On the surface, everything seemed normal, but for whatever reason, Haven's ovaries simply decided they no longer wanted to drop eggs even though they produced them just fine. More than one option was offered—they tried every single one to no avail and with no baby yet.

Here they were now.

IVF.

One last time.

"Saying good luck doesn't seem appropriate," Kim murmured.

Haven ran her palm over the dark curls atop her middle child's head, and laughed under her breath. "You know what, it's as good as anything, Kim."

"Well, good luck, then."

Yeah.

They needed it.

THREE

Haven's SUV was already parked in the driveway by the time Andino arrived home, but that wasn't anything unusual. They could both be in the city at the same time, and somehow, his wife would always arrive home before him—*and* she normally grabbed the girls on the way by his parents' place, too.

"Want me to leave the Rolls in the driveway tonight?" Nate asked from the front.

Andino sighed, considering it. Sometimes he had the enforcer keep the car parked at his home, and other times, he asked for it to go somewhere else. That way, less people knew he was at home and the hours he liked to keep.

One couldn't be too cautious.

"Where's your car?"

"Well—"

Andino chuckled. "Drive the Rolls home, but if you get it back here tomorrow with a fucking scratch, Nate, I swear to *God* ..."

"It'll be in the driveway waiting for you tomorrow morning in perfect condition, boss."

Yeah, it better.

He didn't have to say it out loud.

Just as Andino was about to exit the car, a call rang through to the Bluetooth.

"It's John," Nate said, glancing in the rearview.

"Put it through to my phone—don't leave until I'm in the house."

"Got it."

Despite the fact that Andino frequently and severely missed Pink working for him—he thought he would never get an enforcer as good as that man—Nate wasn't so bad. When it was just him and the guy, he was a lot more tolerable, too. That said good things for him even if Andino wasn't willing to admit those things to the man.

It was what it was.

Andino didn't plan to change.

And ... well, he never really told Pink he missed him although they crossed paths regularly given that the man acted as John's underboss now. He didn't think it needed to be explicitly said considering the fact that Pink had worked for Andino for well over a goddamn decade.

Times changed.

It always did.

"John," Andino greeted into his phone as he stepped out of the Rolls. The first thing that caught his attention was all of his girls' toys scattered over the front lawn. Haven liked to let their daughters play out some of the excess energy from long drives before they went into the house, and he suspected that was the culprit for the mess. "What are you up to, cousin?"

Home is where my heart is.

That was the only thought running through Andino's mind as he took his time to pick up a few toys and carrying them over to the cedar chest on the front porch where they kept them stored. He had a lot of roles to play in his life, but his favorite ones revolved around this home and the people within it. Haven gave him everything, and he didn't think he told her that nearly enough. He made a mental note to do it more often.

"How'd that meeting go?" John asked.

Andino laughed under his breath, replying, "It didn't. Mr. Moshka sent some lower fuck in his place, and instead of calling me to say he didn't want to attend personally, had the *fuck* call to say it would be him I was meeting with. I'm not playing those games."

"Someone calls in to speak with the boss—"

"I better be speaking with a goddamn boss," Andino grunted. "Exactly. Why is this so hard for people to understand?"

"They're not Cosa Nostra?"

Well ...

"You have a point but that changes nothing for me."

"If we don't have standards," John murmured, "then we'll have none, won't we?"

Basically.

It was the only rule Andino cared to follow a lot of the time because as his uncle, Dante, liked to point out pretty regularly ... he broke every single other one that was put in his path just because he could. Or he bent them far enough that they were no longer recognizable. Andino liked to think he made their *famiglia* better for it, too.

Andino went back to the yard for another round of toys, noting that Nate had yet to back out and leave the driveway—as he had been told; the boss wasn't inside the house yet. "I passed along the message that there wouldn't be another chance at a meeting. I'm fine with that decision. I hate people who waste my time."

His greatest pet peeve.

"Or you could pass the name and business venture along to Dante—get his opinion on the situation and if he thinks it might be worth making an exception," John suggested. "It's not a bad thing to get someone else's opinion on these things sometimes."

"John—"

"I'm just saying."

Andino sighed. "How about you handle your side of the city, and I will handle mine?"

His cousin chuckled. "Fine."

He offered John that respect.

Now.

He expected the same back.

"You do you, man," John said.

Andino smiled. "Always do."

"Andino!"

At the call of his name, Andino lifted his attention away from the cedar chest where he was dropping in the last armful of toys from the yard. The box was basically a mix of pink balls, purple and yellow jump ropes, a few dolls that had seen far better days and more toys that frankly, were well-loved by his girls.

Across the road standing on the sidewalk where he watered a row of small hedges stood one of Andino's closest neighbors. And by *close*, he didn't mean friends. The man's four-level home was simply located across the road from Andino's gated driveway that led up to his large property and mansion.

"Maxwell," Andino greeted with a wave.

That was about all he cared to do in response to the neighbor. It wasn't like he made an effort to be active in his upscale suburb. He liked the place for the safety it offered his children, the quiet nature of the community, and the fact he blended in considering who he was and all.

He didn't want to make friends.

"Are you ever gonna get your boy? All that girl stuff must have you going crazy some days over there," the neighbor called.

So loudly, in fact, that even John heard it on the call.

For the first time in longer than Andino cared to admit, he had nothing to say in response to that. He hated to say it, but that wasn't even the tenth time someone had made an ignorant comment about the fact he had three daughters and no sons.

It never bothered him.

He'd never thought about it. Shit, had he only wanted boys when it came to kids, he and Haven would have stopped after their second girl, but *surely* after their third. It just wasn't something that crossed his mind. And when people pointed out the fact that he only had girls, it made him think they assumed his girls weren't worth as much or that he didn't love them as much as he should *because* they weren't boys.

They couldn't be more wrong.

"Andi," John started to say.

Andino turned his back to the neighbor where he stood on the porch, not even caring to respond to the man. He usually didn't when nonsense like this happened. "Haven and the girls are waiting for me— we'll chat tomorrow, yeah?"

John let out a hard breath. "He's just another asshole, man."

"Yeah, I know."

Didn't mean Andino wouldn't get him back for it, though.

Someday.

Today wasn't that day.

Instead of worrying about that, he hung up his call and headed inside the house. The second he opened the front door, three pairs of feet came stomping his way. His girls shouted *daddy*. He didn't even get his shoes off before three little arms wrapped around him like bars.

Andino didn't mind.

In fact, he loved it.

He greeted each of his girls—Lynn, Rose, and Emily—with a hug and kiss to the tops of their curly heads. He made sure to ask about their day and everything—each second—he had missed when he was away from them. The same way he did any other day. His little *principessas*. Perfect in every fucking way. Half of him and half of their mother. These girls were his whole world alongside their ma.

"Missed you, Daddy."

"Love you, Daddy."

Yeah, this was definitely the best part of his day.

FOUR

Haven just finished scrubbing her kitchen sink until it sparkled before she moved on to attacking her counters, too. Spraying them down with thick, foamy cleaner, she grabbed the rag and started wiping them down.

From the table, Andino cleared his throat in his captain chair. "Do you want me to help or—"

"You're fine where you are."

She didn't even look away from her work. With the girls in bed and the day almost over, Haven needed to get all her energy and stress out of her mind, or she was never going to fall asleep. That's just how her mind did things, and she wouldn't apologize for it. After all these years being married, Andino knew how her nights worked.

"Okay," her husband murmured. "How was your day?"

"Busy. My meeting at the club went well. The new policies went over pretty good with everybody, so that's one less issue for me to worry about. The girls didn't give your mother any trouble, and they tired your father out."

"Did you miss the traffic at noon?"

"Hit the tail end of it."

"Of course," he muttered.

"Same as every other day. What about you?"

Andino grunted something she couldn't understand. Glancing up from her wide wipes of the counter, she found him staring out the bay window of their kitchen. It wasn't as though there was anything interesting to watch out there. A dark yard—a few trees.

Interesting.

Yet, she had to admit that he looked damn good sitting in his chair with the sleeves of his dress shirt rolled up around his elbows, the top two buttons undone, and his tie lost somewhere. She would probably find it on the floor between this room and one of the girls' bedrooms because he was the one who put them all to bed and read them their nightly stories.

They loved their daddy.

Haven did, too.

More than she could explain.

"What was that?" she asked.

Andino glanced over at her with a sheepish smile— something he *rarely* did, and she quite liked the sight of it all the same. "Sorry. I said my day didn't go as planned, that's all."

"Oh?"

He shrugged. "But I like listening to you talk about yours more even if you are stress cleaning while you do it."

Haven grinned.

That would be Andino.

Just calling her out like that.

"What's wrong?" he asked, his tone soft.

"Well, nothing, really."

He arched a brow. A good sign that he didn't believe a single word that was coming out of her mouth and wouldn't mind telling her exactly that, either.

"Okay, *nothing*," Haven said, "as in nothing should be wrong, right? Look at our life, Andino. Look at everything we have and who we are and how lucky we are. Why would anything be wrong? I should be grateful, not—"

"Having privilege doesn't mean you're not human, Haven."

She let out a heavy breath.

Why did he have to be right?

"What's wrong?" he asked again. "The truth this time, you know?"

She made quick work of drying the counter before she tossed the rag aside and rested her palms along the edge. Staring at her husband across the room, she thought about every little thing that had been weighing on her mind since she received the call from the specialist's clinic about their next round of IVF.

"We'll be starting the final round of IVF soon—I got the call today."

Andino's smile grew. "Okay."

"But we're clear on this, right? It's the *last* time, Andi. I don't want to do it again."

Sometimes, it was devastating in the way that they could be *so sure* it had happened—she had to be pregnant—only to find out that it didn't take. Why, if her body was so healthy, and she had managed to produce three children—a fourth pregnancy had ended in a D & C because it was ectopic—without any medical intervention, was this so difficult now? It made Haven feel a lot of things about herself that *hurt*. And she didn't want to keep struggling like that with every new round.

"It's the last one," he agreed. "Whatever you want, I told you that."

She let out a slow breath, but stayed quiet.

Andino didn't miss it.

"That's not what's wrong, though, is it?"

"No," she admitted. "Part of it, I suppose."

Andino waited her out.

29

Haven felt silly.

"I get in this headspace where I feel like I can't talk about the IVF or anything else," she said.

"Why?"

How simple that question was. The answer was anything but. It went right back to what she already said.

"Because look at our life, Andino. We have three children. There are people who don't even have one child. People who have struggled for *years*. Who've done what we've been doing for a lot longer than we have. And I just … sometimes I wonder if people look at us and think we should just be grateful for what we have."

After her rant, Haven fell silent. Apparently, her husband didn't like that because he stood from the table, slow and graceful despite his large size. Picking up his glass, now empty of water, he carried it to the sink and placed it inside before he came up behind Haven. He fit in at her back perfectly, the hard lines of his chest molding against her softer ones. His mouth found the back of her neck; he kissed the ink coloring her skin there, and the newest one under her right ear that was just a simple cursive *A*.

For him.

Because of course she would imprint him permanently on her body. He was already her entire heart and soul. What did a little ink on her skin matter?

"We wanted more children, didn't we?" he murmured against her skin.

"Yes."

"And we struggled after Emily to be able to do that without help, yeah?"

"Yeah, but—"

"We have the means to have another child, and more than enough love to share, Haven. We *want* another child, and we're doing what we need to do to have that child. Nobody gets to make you feel guilty for that."

She let out a shaky breath.

He smiled against her skin.

"Now, let me take you to bed."

"*You're terrible.*"

"In the best way," he agreed.

Her heart thundered. "Take me to bed, then."

He did as she wanted, cradling her in his arms as he carried her up the stairs and down the hallway to their master bedroom with ease. She loved nothing more than the sight of her husband undressing her with his hands and his eyes and his *mind*. It was like she could see in his eyes all the lovely, *sinful* things he planned to do to her the very second he had her naked and under him in their bed.

Her next favorite thing was to watch him undress while she spread her thighs wide and showed him every inch of her that was only his. He made her wet just by being close. She shivered and sighed when he came a little closer to see her fingers roving through her slit. That pleased hum of his when he kneeled between her widened legs with his cock hard under fast strokes of his hand had her vibrating with need.

He ate her first.

Hungry.

Crazy.

Until she was flying high.

And then he fucked her the way she loved the most—on her knees, her face and chest pushed to the bed by his hands, while he nailed her hard from behind until she was whining with another orgasm and feeling like she couldn't breathe.

Nothing had to matter when they were like that.

Nothing at all.

FIVE

"Babe."

"Hmm?"

Andino shot Haven a grin from the driver's seat. "We're here."

For the first time since they left their home that morning, much earlier than they normally would to beat traffic and be where they needed to be with time to spare, Haven looked away from the passenger window like she had just noticed their surroundings. While she couldn't see the tall buildings outside the parking garage, he knew she would recognize where they were well enough considering how many times he'd used this since they started coming to the specialist's clinic.

"Oh," Haven murmured.

"You good?"

Her gaze met his, and he swore that every emotion she felt stared back at him in those moments. *No*, he didn't think his wife was one hundred percent okay, but who would be when they were about to go in to begin another weeks-long round of IVF that, so far, had yet to lead them down a path that ended with a baby.

It was exhausting.

Emotionally draining.

Even he knew that.

"I'm just tired," Haven said, shrugging one shoulder.

He didn't really need her to explain. Not when he knew exactly what she meant all too well. He also didn't think his wife wanted him to list all the reasons why they could and should do this again, so instead, he leaned over in the seat after unbuckling to get closer to her. She turned her head more toward him when his palm found the soft warmth of her neck. The pad of his thumb traced lines over the colorful ink that peeked out beneath the collar of her jacket, and then up to the cursive *A* and the little star behind her ear.

Haven's small shiver and sweet sigh from his touch had Andino wishing they'd spent just a little more time in bed the last week—but fuck, even that was monitored and dictated by doctors far more than he wanted to admit.

"I love you, Haven," he murmured.

She smiled. "And I love you."

"If you want to call this off—"

"I don't."

Andino chuckled. "*Okay*, but anytime you do, babe, you just say the word. The girls are *always* going to be enough."

She dragged in a breath, and met his gaze before staring over his shoulder at the waiting bank of elevators. The middle would take them up to the clinic. Soon, they needed to be out of their vehicle and heading inside if they didn't want to miss their appointment. The clinic didn't make exceptions for those who were late.

"This is it—one last time, Andino."

He nodded. "All right, one last time."

"All right," the doctor said, sitting back in the chair to flip another page in his folder while he crossed his legs. "And we went over everything, didn't we, Joan?"

The nurse gave Andino and Haven a sympathetic smile from the side. "We did—policy, sorry. We know you've gone through this more than once before."

"Ah, there was something else we needed to discuss."

The man's finger tapped on the top of whatever paper he found interesting before he looked their way again. He tipped the paper up for the nurse to see. She nodded and murmured her confirmation as well on it all.

The private room was comfortable and *comforting*, one of the things Andino liked about it. Like much of the rest of the clinic, it was stark white right down to the furniture inside it. The walls, like many of the others in the clinic, were covered with family photos and newborn shots. Some had notes attached, others had notes written right *on* the photographs. All from families who had come here for help.

Andino couldn't say, and didn't know, whether or not—if they were even successful—that his child's photograph would join the ranks. It wasn't something he gave much thought to, and he didn't think now was the right time to do it, either.

"And what's that?" Haven asked.

"For one—we have three frozen embryos left from the two of you. So, unless we're planning to do another retrieval, which neither of you wanted, we're left with them to implant on procedure day. So, I want to confirm you don't want to go ahead with another round to store more embryos."

Haven glanced over at Andino.

No, they did not want to do that again.

Besides, if this round was successful, that would leave the remaining embryos left to store or donate what they gained from a second retrieval process. He understood very well that there were people who needed donated embryos for their own infertility journeys, but he didn't think that neither him, nor Haven, were willing to do that. They'd already talked about it. They also didn't want to store embryos. They couldn't just destroy them when it was all said and done, either.

"We'll go with what we have," Andino said for his wife. "And we won't be doing another retrieval whether this round of IVF is successful or not."

"Three is still a good number for procedure day," the doctor assured. "Before, you hadn't asked to know the sexes of the embryos, but do you want to now?"

Andino let Haven decide that.

He'd never cared.

"Sure," she said quietly.

"All males this time. Most were."

Huh.

"And one more thing," the doctor continued, but this time, he only looked at Haven when he spoke.

"Knowing that you've had three successful pregnancies on your own without intervention, and a fourth that ended up ectopic—which caused a removal of your right fallopian tube—and now this … With the unexplained infertility, if you've settled on the decision not to have more children, then you should seriously consider sterilization."

The suggestion came *kindly.*

Andino understood why the doctor brought it up, too. Even the doctor who had handled the births of their other children and was the one to diagnose Haven's ectopic pregnancy had said the same thing. It was just as much about preventing something from happening again as it was taking control of their life, essentially.

It still felt like a punch.

Haven told the doctor simply, "We'll have to think about that."

SIX

"What if the final round doesn't work?"

Haven's quiet question had her best friend falling into silence beside her. Well, *one* of her best friends. She'd already spent a good portion of the night before crying in the phone to Valeria who promised she was going to make time to come to New York during the upcoming week because they needed *girl time*.

Val wasn't wrong.

Today, though, Catherine sat beside her. They'd invited Siena, but she ended up running Lucky to the hospital because he had a high fever. It was always something with kids.

Catherine reached over, and snuck an arm around Haven's shoulders. She said nothing as the two of them leaned closer together and watched their kids navigate the park's play equipment. For the moment, it felt like exactly what Haven needed. Usually, it would be Andino comforting her when she dared to show that little bit of vulnerability about their current IVF journey, but he was somewhere across the city playing *boss*.

Haven only had her friend.

Catherine wasn't so bad.

"Is it weird," Haven started, "that even though I know being done after this round is the right thing to do for us, I'm still sad about it?"

"Well ..."

"Give it to me straight. You always do."

Catherine laughed, and bumped her shoulder with Haven's. The two women let one another go and resumed their previous sitting position on the bench overlooking the park. "I mean, honestly, after Nazio ... we were done, too, but I was still sad about it. And then everything that he did for the first time, I knew it was the *last* first time a baby of mine would ever do that. Not to mention, when he stopped doing something, you know?"

"Except …"

"Hmm?"

Haven looked over at Catherine. "That would mean Emily was my last baby—she wasn't supposed to be the last one. I didn't take the time to notice all those *last* first things, or even when—"

"*Haven*."

She stopped her rambling instantly, and dragged in a burning lungful of air. She knew it was partly the stress of the whole situation, meds that she had to take for this process to have its best chance at succeeding, and just … *hormones* in general. That was all making her more emotional than she would normally be and willing to share.

Not that it mattered.

She couldn't control it.

"You're a great mom," Catherine said, "and you know it."

"But—"

"No buts. Not about this."

Haven found her three girls near the swings. Lynn, their oldest, was currently helping Emily climb up to a

43

large slide while Rose stood at the rear in her cute yellow dress. All of her daughters were kind, *oh*, so sweet, and perfect. They were everything she wanted and more. Somehow, and though they were still young, she had managed to raise some pretty decent humans so far.

"If it doesn't work," Haven said, settling herself on the chance that it might not, "then I'll be okay. We'll be just fine."

Catherine nodded with a smile. "Yeah, I think so, too."

"But it's still okay to be sad, right?"

"Absolutely. Nobody gets to tell you how to feel, Haven."

She would remember that. *Definitely.*

Haven had just finished buckling in the last of her children and closed the door of the SUV when a man rounded the front of the Mercedes. She might not have noticed him on another day—there were often *many* people at the park on any given day, and they usually were a good mix of different kinds of people, too.

Some had kids.

Some jogged.

There was even a dog park.

Andino used to like that for Snaps, but the rescued pit bull had fallen ill the year before due to age-related complications that he hadn't been able to pull out of at the end of it. He hadn't suffered, which was one of the only things they were grateful for about the pup's passing, because everything else about it had been fucking heartbreaking.

Still was, really.

It wasn't unusual to see a man wearing all black— from his tie to the shined shoes on his feet—in the park. Hell, Haven had met her husband in a park just like this where he walked his mean-looking dog while wearing a suit.

But this strange man?

He looked right *at* her.

Not like a passing glance, or even like it was the first time he'd seen her face. No, he stared at her as though he knew exactly who she was and that he had something to say to her.

Haven looked over her shoulder as the man came closer to the rear end of the Mercedes where she'd just shut her kids into the back—where were her enforcers? Did she even need them?

Something told her she *did*.

Maybe it was the aura the man gave off.

She didn't really know.

But something was *wrong*.

"Haven Marcello," the man said, not even posing it as a question. "I have a message to pass along to you, and then I'll be on my way."

Her hand slipped inside the bag at her side, and she palmed the small handgun that she always kept on-hand because Andino made it very clear she didn't have a choice. The same way she didn't get an option on whether or not her enforcers would follow close behind daily.

So, where the fuck were they?

"What do you want?" Haven asked.

She'd just grabbed tight to the gun, readying to pull it out.

The man's next words stopped her.

"Tell your husband that Mr. Moshka would like another meeting. It's not a request."

What?

She didn't get the chance to ask.

The man turned and left.

SEVEN

"They had guns pointed at him, boss," Nate said.

Andino nodded, but continued to stare over the front property of his home. Darkness had come, cloaking everything in blackness that matched the current undertones of his mind and soul. There was never a time when the mafia wouldn't touch someone if they were *in* the life—it didn't matter if he was the most powerful man in New York with a hundred guards on constant watch, these things would *always* happen.

It was just a matter of when, why, and how.

He had most of those answers this time which was better than he could say for other times. Did it make this any easier or would he be able to go inside and calm his wife's nerves? That she had been raging on and off for the last several hours?

Absolutely not.

Yet …

Andino chose this life.

All of it.

"My wife still didn't see her guards," he noted. "Which is part of the problem. How close were they to Haven and the girls that she couldn't even see them when she needed them?"

Nate cleared his throat, and glanced over his shoulder. Andino didn't miss the way the man shifted from foot to foot, either. A damn good sign of the man's nerves. He was Andino's best enforcer, and one he trusted the *very* most ever since Pink had moved onto other things. Because of that, he tended to take note of things that made Nate tick.

"What aren't you saying?"

The enforcer sighed. "It's what I don't want to say—I'd rather not offend my boss. Not only do you sign my paychecks, but you also get gun happy when people piss you off."

Well ...

"Just say it," Andino muttered, giving the man a look from the side.

"She was scared. The girls were there and all. It was just her. She *rarely* notices her enforcers anymore anyway, which was what *you* wanted. For her to feel as normal as possible while she went about her day, right?"

Andino let out a hard breath, already knowing where this was going. "*And?*"

Nate cleared his throat. "She probably had tunnel vision—focused in on the threat. It's what most people do in that situation. Hell, she couldn't even tell you what color the car was that was parked beside her own. *Tunnel vision.*"

"And all of this leads to you telling me what, exactly?"

The man shrugged his shoulders under his leather jacket. "Listen, I know you're pissed and all, boss, but I don't think you should go off on the boys for today. They did their job. They *escorted* the guy out of there only to find out he was a paid messenger. He didn't even have a weapon on him. They're good enforcers."

They were.

Usually.

Andino didn't want to argue that.

"What makes you think my first reaction is to punish the enforcers who were watching her today?" Andino asked, honesty curious.

For a few reasons …

Nate gave him a look. "It's your wife, man. And your *girls*. Anything happens to them, and you see fucking red. We all know it. And those guys? They're terrified of it."

Hmm.

Andino nodded. "Good to know. Keep an eye on the house, yeah?"

"Got it, boss."

The enforcer waited until Andino had opened the front door and stepped inside before he exited the safety of the porch and headed out onto the walkway. Andino wasn't sure where Nate would stay on the property for the evening. Sometimes he just walked around the property line, and other times he sat in a car. It wasn't every night that Andino required Nate to watch the house, but on a night like this one?

Yep. Other nights, someone else did it.

Not tonight.

After Andino closed the front door and toed off his leather loafers, he heard the first slam of a cupboard door. A hard sigh left him as he shoved his hands in his pockets, stared up at the ceiling of the entryway to his home, and took a moment just to breathe and think. The girls were all in bed and none the wiser about what had happened today. Both he and Haven made sure of that—if he had any say, it would be a good many years before his daughters knew the truth of who he was and their life.

Tonight was not the night.

"Are you just going to stand there?" Haven asked sharply.

God.

The last thing Andino wanted to do was fight with his wife. Or rather, let her rage at him because she was scared and didn't know how to handle it.

"Haven—"

"You still haven't even told me what all that was about today!"

"Because it doesn't matter," he returned, finally meeting her gaze. "And it'll only piss you off even more than you already are. Does that seem like a smart route to go down to you?"

"You're an asshole."

Yep.

No news was good news, he supposed.

"I'm going to handle it, Haven. It won't happen again. I promise."

She looked like every inch the hurricane she truly could be. Tattooed, beautiful, *angry,* and entirely his.

"He got past my enforcers," she said softly.

Yeah, and that was the real problem.

"And the girls were there," she added.

It would not matter to his wife that the guy who accosted her at the park was practically harmless considering he didn't even have a weapon on him when it happened. All that mattered to Haven was that it happened in the first place.

He understood that well enough.

It pissed him off, too.

Andino nodded. "I'll handle it."

Before his wife could reply or start another argument—it really depended on which way her mood swung, frankly—a cry from one of their girls echoed overtop their heads. Both of them looked upward at the sound.

Being parents never stopped.

Not for anything.

"I have to make a call," Andino said, "but then I'll be up to help."

Haven gave him another one of those looks—one that stung like nothing else. "Whatever, Andino."

He understood her anger.

She could have it.

John was the person Andino called first. As soon as his cousin picked up the call, he muttered, "Did you hear the news about what happened today at the park?"

"Unfortunately," John muttered. "What are you going to do about that?"

"Handle it."

"How?"

"That's why I called you. I need a plan."

John chuckled. "I love making those."

Yeah, he knew.

EIGHT

"And the pretty little unicorn flew away …"

Haven leaned her head against the doorjamb of their master bedroom, listening to her husband down the hall reading yet another bedtime story to Rose because their middle child just did not want to go to bed. It wasn't as though she had nightmares, and since the kid didn't even know what had happened that day, it couldn't be anxiety from that, either.

Certainly not what her mother was currently feeling.

No, the girl was just impossible to put to bed. Even when she was younger, Haven swore Rose would switch her days and nights around from week to week. As a toddler, she rarely had a proper nap which often led to a clingy, grumpy little girl they still loved no matter what.

And then there was Andino …

Rose *loved* her daddy. All he needed to do was give her five minutes of his attention, like reading a nighttime story, and the girl would be snoring away sooner rather than later.

On another night, Haven would have enjoyed listening to Andino read to one of their daughters. It was the quickest way to make her heart swell with *every* emotion possible that was good and great and wonderful. All the love in their home was everything she dreamed of, and her girls had the *best* father.

Except right now, she felt none of that.

How could she when she was scared?

The bigger problem was that Haven didn't know how to explain that to Andino, and she couldn't be like him, either. She wasn't capable of being a mother in one moment, pretending everything was perfectly fine, and then flip a switch to be the kind of woman who just doesn't bat an eye at something like what happened that day.

She couldn't do it.

She wouldn't apologize for it, either.

Not that he ever asked her to.

Shaking her head, but not getting free of the heaviness weighing her down like nothing else, Haven began to ready for the night. She had no doubt that once Andino was done with Rose, they wouldn't have to run for one of the girls again for the rest of the night. Changing from her day clothes into one of Andino's shirts that were *huge* on her, she then sat down at her vanity to begin removing her makeup and the rest of this godforsaken day.

Even after she finished her nightly routine, Haven still didn't move from her vanity. Instead, she hugged her arms around her middle and knees once she drew her feet up to the edge of the chair. She stared at the reflection in the mirror, letting her thoughts race through her mind one after another, warring for space and attention, while she did nothing more than watch the battle in her eyes. Soon, a familiar figure stood behind her in the mirror.

"Did you not hear the phone?" he asked.

Haven rested her chin on her arm. "Did it ring?"

"Yeah, it was your mom. She said they got their tickets for that trip here in a couple months."

A slow, steady stream of air left her lips in a long sigh.

Andino kneeled down as he put his hands to her chair. A soft kiss found the back of her neck while he murmured all the words she needed to hear—words she *loved* to hear him say. It wasn't any different than the things he'd been telling her all day or even the shit he said downstairs. *He would fix it. He was sorry. It wouldn't happen again.*

She didn't doubt it.

She also knew it very well might happen all over again—time and time again, in fact, over their life together. Because that was the thing. This was their life. The one *she* decided to spend with him. Still, knowing all those things and settling herself with those facts didn't change that Haven could never prepare for these days.

"I just …"

His lips hesitated against the soft, sensitive skin behind her ear when her words trailed off. Lifting his gaze to meet hers in the mirror, he arched a brow to silently urge her to continue. It took her a moment, but she did. *Somehow.*

"I just don't know how to be the person who has moments like those happen and doesn't bat a lash at it, and then can turn around and be a mom and a business owner and a *wife*. It's a little too much. I always fuck up at something, don't I?"

"Do you?" he asked.

"Andino—"

"I'm not sure what you want to hear from me here, Haven."

"How do you be that man so well—how am I supposed to always be that woman, too?"

"I don't have an answer."

"At all, or just right now?" she returned.

"I just do it—I just *am*."

"But *why*?"

"I don't know."

He would eventually give her an answer. She knew it—it simply might take some time.

Haven tipped her head a little to the side, letting him go back to loving her neck with soft kisses that had lust swelling in her gut and heat traveling straight down to the spot between her thighs. Right now, she needed that, too.

Him.

Closeness.

Them.

He gave her that, too.

Like everything else.

Sometimes, she had to be patient enough to wait for it, though.

NINE

John's voice rang through the Bluetooth of Andino's Rolls-Royce as he parked in a familiar parking lot. "Bit early for you to be calling, isn't it? I didn't think you rolled your ass out of bed before ten anymore, man."

Andino scoffed at that. "I have three kids—*girls*, by the way, in case you forgot. Two of which think they need to be up making as much noise as possible in my bathroom because they won't even use their own. Their mother's makeup isn't in there. Oh, and the youngest one? I think she wakes up at the ass crack of dawn every morning. Before *ten*. Right. Don't joke with me today. It's not one of those."

On the other end of the line, his cousin chuckled. That was probably the only reason Andino didn't default straight to his usual asshole mode. He knew John was only trying to lighten him up—one of the few people that knew what today was and how important it was to Andino and Haven.

"You and Siena are still good to grab the girls from Mom and Dad's place later, right?" he asked, eyeing the empty row of seats in the back of his vehicle. Usually, they would be filled with empty car seats, but he left those at his parents. "I dropped them off about an hour ago."

And took his time saying goodbye.

Hugs and kisses for each of his girls.

Andino didn't mention that.

"Absolutely," John replied. "We planned to grab them right before lunch, make it an afternoon, and bring them home when they're too tired to think."

Andino laughed. "Sounds good."

"Yeah, and uh, hey … about today?"

"What about it?"

He found his reflection in the rearview mirror as he waited. The thing about Andino that a lot of people didn't really know was that, when needed, he could put on a good front. Today was one of those days. He figured that his wife had enough stress and worry of her own about what was going on that he really didn't need to add to it with his own. So, just by looking at him, one couldn't tell that his stomach was in knots and his chest grew heavy with every breath, but he was also fine with that.

"Good luck, man," John said quietly.

Andino dragged in a heavy breath. "Yeah, thanks."

They were going to need it.

Once he'd hung up the call with John, Andino cut the engine on the car and glanced sideways to stare at the sign on the brick building. *The Haven*, it read. Written in hot pink neon lights that weren't currently turned on, the sign had been one of the few things his wife decided to carry on from her old club to the new one.

He rarely came here.

Frankly, he knew better.

Haven didn't work as many nights at the club as she used to—if there were issues that needed handled or paperwork, she came in during the day, called meetings, or whatever else. She also had two managers and an accountant that handled business for her. He knew sometimes that bothered her when she wanted to be more hands-on than she actually was.

But that came with being a mom.

And a wife.

Not that it mattered or made a difference. The club was just as successful as her previous one. There wasn't the same draw for patrons—it wasn't a strip joint; not that he would have said anything one way or another. Yet, the place managed to draw in a wide crowd from various backgrounds and ages.

Shit.

Even he couldn't do that.

However, despite the fact he tried to give Haven and her business a wide berth of space—then it never looked like her club was anything *but* her club—he didn't think she would mind that he was there today. Stepping out of his vehicle, Andino fixed his blazer and scanned the surrounding parking lot and side street.

Mostly empty.

A quiet city day.

Nothing out of the ordinary.

The enforcers that would usually keep an eye on Andino from a safe distance weren't even anywhere to be seen, but that was by his own choice. Even his wife's enforcer wouldn't be following them around today.

It was a private thing.

Procedure day.

Turning back to the car, Andino *almost* thought to open the rear door to let his pup out. Sometimes, though Snaps hadn't been on one of these rides in over a year since his passing, Andino caught himself behaving as though his old companion was still around. He missed his dog like nobody would ever know.

Especially in these moments.

Sighing, he decided to leave the car running as he headed for the club. Certainly no one would bother it here—he might not come around, but that didn't mean people weren't aware of just who he was when he did show up.

Inside the club, Andino found the place quiet and lit up. Chairs rested on tables while the hardwood floors gleamed underneath, freshly waxed. All the neon signs inside were also turned off, the DJ booth had been shut down, and the bar was empty. The few workers who came in during the day to clean, stock the bar, and whatever else barely even noticed Andino passing them by.

That was fine.

He wasn't their boss.

Soon, he found his wife inside her office. Flipping through what looked to be an order sheet, Haven didn't even look up from her work as she said, "Remember, your managers are the ones you need to deal with if you need—"

"But I don't work here, babe."

A smile crept over her pretty lips. Haven's head tipped up, and her gaze landed on him where he leaned in her doorway. Her stare drifted down over him, taking in his three-piece suit and settling on the grin playing at his mouth.

"Hey," he murmured.

Haven smiled a little wider. "Hey yourself."

"You busy?"

"Aren't we always?"

She made a good point.

Shifting to stand straight without leaning, Andino shoved his hands into his pockets and gave his wife a wink from the doorway. There was something about the sight of her in a black pencil skirt, heels that made her legs look fantastic, and a loose blouse that hinted at her cleavage while she worked behind a desk that made him want to cross the office and show her every wicked thought in his mind at the moment.

He didn't, though.

Couldn't.

"I thought you might want a drive to the clinic," Andino said, "instead of us just meeting up there today."

Haven gave him a look. "I thought you had work to do today?"

"Cleared most of it away. This is more important. I can take a day."

"I love you, Andino."

Yeah.

He loved her, too.

More than she would ever know.

TEN

"Here, let me help you—"

"I got it," Haven whispered.

The nurse gave her a small smile, but nodded all the same and backed off to let Haven climb up on the uncomfortable procedure table on her own. The table with the stirrups ready for her feet and a view of the wall of mirrors opposite to her current position. Those mirrors were a lie, though, because she knew they were windows into the procedure room for the doctor and other staff that would be involved today.

"We've gone over the checklist, so you know everything that's going to happen from here," the nurse said, "but the doctor did want to confirm a few things that we'd spoken about at your last appointment."

Haven laid back on the table—or did they consider it a bed?—and stared up at the ceiling overhead. "Now?"

"We can wait until after, if you'd prefer."

Well ...

"Let's just get it over with," she replied.

Then, her husband would come in.

They could get this started.

"You're firm on this being the last round, correct?"

Haven let out a shaky exhale. "Yes."

"You were informed that the embryos we'll be implanting today are—"

"Yes."

The nurse glanced up—Haven caught it out of the corner of her eye but didn't bother to turn and look straight on at the woman. What did it matter?

They had done this already.

Many times.

She was tired of the same fucking questions. *Exhausted* from the lack of results. Stressed out to the goddamn max about this day because it was the last one. Excuse her for not wanting to go through yet another round of questions and answers that had already been asked and answered.

"Would you like your husband to come in, now?" the nurse asked, her tone softer.

Haven nodded but said nothing.

"Okay. I'll go get him."

"Thank you."

Before long, Andino came to sit on the stool beside Haven's bed. He rested his chin on her arm while his fingers found hers and wrapped tight. She turned her head and caught his gaze. His little smile had her answering it with her own.

"Hey," she whispered.

That gaze of his—always so intense and full of love when it leveled on her—took her to an entirely different place. She loved him for that.

More than she could explain.

"Hey," he replied.

"One last time, right?"

Andino nodded. "One last time, babe. I was thinking …"

"Do you do that often?"

72

He bared his teeth, muttering, "Smart ass."

She was.

And he loved it, too.

"What were you thinking?"

"Giovanni Andino," he said. "For a name."

Right.

Because if this worked, they were guaranteed a boy. Wasn't that what the doctor had said at their last appointment? All the embryos left were genetically male.

"I like that," Haven said. "Might be more than one."

Her husband chuckled. "Giovanni for the first, then."

A flutter of worry slipped through Haven's heart. "But what if—"

"No buts. No *what ifs*. None of it."

She let out a hard breath.

Andino leaned in and kissed her cheek. It was enough to settle the raging war of emotions in her heart. People couldn't possibly know unless they were the ones going through the same thing as her, but this wasn't easy.

Not on the mind.

The body.

Or the heart.

Nothing about infertility was *easy*.

"Giovanni Andino," he told her. "No matter what."

Haven nodded. "No matter what."

That would be his name.

ELEVEN

"Daddy?"

Andino glanced up from the rim of the glass of cognac he'd been swirling and sipping to see his oldest daughter lingering just beyond his office doorway. A smile crept over his lips as her big eyes grew wide, and in silent question, she raised the item in her hands for him to see a little better.

A book.

"Would you?" Lynn asked.

Shit.

She didn't even need to ask, really.

"Yeah, baby, of course. Come here."

"Yay," Lynn crowed before she sped across his office. He couldn't even hear the pattering of her feet; that's how quiet she was. "Thanks, Daddy."

"Always," he told her.

His arms were already open to pull his oldest daughter into his lap. Her sisters were probably still sleeping soundly in their bed. He swore from the time Lynn learned to talk *and* walk, and they could no longer contain her to a crib because she became big enough to move into a toddler bed. His girl constantly came to look for him at night. More than once, she crawled into bed between her mother and father.

"You know," Andino told her, resting his chin on the top of her head while he situated the book in front of them, so he could see it well enough to read, "someday, you might have to read yourself a book— what will you do then?"

"Why wouldn't you read it for me?"

"Well, you'd be able to read it yourself."

"But I like it when *you* read it, Daddy."

Andino grinned, and then kissed Lynn on the top of her curly head. Hell, he would read her books over video chat when she was away in college if that's what she wanted, but he figured they had time to work all that out. "Daddy will always read to you whenever you ask, I promise."

Tipping her head back so she could stare up at him, Lynn smiled sweetly. "I know."

There were a lot of things people just assumed about Andino based on appearance or what they thought they knew. He was fine with letting them think he was a cold asshole with a heart of stone—it was the ones he loved the most who knew exactly what was truly in Andino's heart and how much he adored them.

Including his little girls.

Resting his cheek along his daughter's head, he started reading the story about the little duck who had somehow managed to get lost from the pond.

Very quietly, he heard Lynn whisper, "I love you, Daddy."

"Love you, too, baby."

Before his kids came along, he never gave the topic of children much thought at all. That was, until he met and married Haven. Then, the only thing on his mind had been starting a life with her—which just happened to include kids.

Their family felt full.

Still, not yet complete.

He loved it anyway.

He loved it *either* way.

Andino knew how lucky he was.

After he'd finished Lynn's book, he let his daughter stay tucked on his lap. He even grabbed the afghan blanket his wife left on the back of his office chair as decoration to cover her up with while they scrolled through a couple of her favorite shows on his desktop. Despite the fact he had a guest coming and it was late, none of that mattered much to him.

Someday, his girls would be older. Spending time with him like this might not be the cool thing to do, and so he would always take advantage when he got the chance.

"Late night with your daddy, *principessa* Lynn?"

At the sound of her grandfather's voice coming from the doorway, Lynn poked her head up out of the blanket to look over the edge of the desk. Andino grinned at his father, too. Giovanni didn't seem to mind the extra guest. His dad still tried to make time to come over once a week so that the two of them could sit down and … well, do anything. Mostly talk.

After all these years—and Andino being a grown ass man—and his father still made time for him that was *only* his. Had they spoiled him? Oh, yes. He thought it might have made him a better man and father in the end, though.

Andino patted Lynn on her head, saying, "She was just heading to bed, weren't you, *bambina*?"

Big eyes looked up at him.

He got the pouty lip, too.

Giovanni chuckled as he took a seat on the opposite side of the desk. "No, actually, it looks like she's probably going to stay right there."

Lynn grinned. "Hey, Grandpapa."

"Hey, sweetheart."

"Watch your show while I talk to Grandpapa," Andino told Lynn. "And when the episode is over, you go back to bed. Deal?"

Lynn thought about it for all of five seconds before settled back against her father under the blanket and muttering, "*Deal*."

"Ah, compromise," Giovanni said, laughing under his breath. "The only way I found to keep your ass under control for *years*."

Andino smirked.

His father wasn't wrong.

The office quieted while Lynn's show continued playing in the background. Giovanni tipped up a glass for Andino to see—one he must have gotten from downstairs. Like his own on the desk, it seemed filled with the twenty-year cognac he kept downstairs.

"Haven grabbed me a drink," his father said. "She seems … quiet."

That had Andino sighing.

"Not surprising. She's been quiet for a couple of weeks."

"Oh?"

"Since the last IVF round—we go for the blood test tomorrow."

Giovanni nodded. "So, tomorrow is the day, hmm?"

"Tomorrow's the day."

"How do you feel?"

That was not an easy question.

And he didn't have an easy answer.

Andino simply settled on saying, "Ready. I'm ready."

Regardless of the outcome.

No matter the rest.

He was ready for it.

It's who he was.

TWELVE

Sitting in a chair beside her husband, Haven rubbed at the spot on her inner elbow where the clinic had drawn blood for the pregnancy test. She hadn't said much leading up to this day—she wanted to be grateful no matter the outcome of their choices regarding this journey—but she was still terrified all the same.

And a part of her hoped this didn't end in sadness.

Andino's hand snagged her arm into his grasp, stopping her fidgeting. She glanced up at the same time he tugged her forward until she sat on the very edge of the chair. Without a word, his thumb found the spot she'd been rubbing for the last ten minutes—now a bluish bruised mess—and he pressed gently before sweeping his digit soothingly over her skin.

"We don't know—don't overthink it yet, Haven."

She let out a shaky sigh.

"How do you know that's what I'm doing?"

He gave her one of *those* grins. His signature grin, she'd call it. The one that—no matter where they were or what they were doing—could make her stomach do the best kind of flip-flops. It probably didn't help that Andino never looked better than he did when he wore one of his three-piece suits, filled it out so well, and seemed as though he didn't have a care in the world. All things that fit his current description. All these years with him, and he still gave her butterflies. This time was no exception.

Damn.

She loved this man.

"I just know you," he settled on saying.

Knowing they probably wouldn't have much more time alone before the doctor came in to deliver the results of their pregnancy test, Haven wanted to take advantage of their privacy. Leaning across the space between their two chairs in the private room, she pressed a kiss to the side of Andino's jaw where his two days worth of scruff tickled her lips.

"Love you," she whispered.

"*Ti amo—sempre, mia Tesoro.*"

Her hand came up to rest against his cheek. Her fingertips pressed into his jaw; it was her way of holding him, of keeping him closer until she was ready to let go. Which lately, seemed like never. Not that Andino *ever* complained.

"It's going to be fine," she heard him say.

All she could do was nod.

She wanted to believe him.

History proved differently, unfortunately.

Yet, all of those doubts and painful memories faded away when Andino cupped Haven's face in his warm palms and tipped her head back so that the two of them could stare at one another. He leaned in closer until his forehead pressed against hers. He kissed her once—softly. Then, twice … with a little more hunger and *love*.

More love.

She'd always need more of that from him.

And then in a blink, Andino pulled her from the chair she'd been using to his own. Or rather, his lap. Those strong arms of his wrapped around her like a security blanket she hadn't known she needed until it was warming and keeping her safe all at the same time.

Well, maybe she didn't need to know what she needed.

Andino always knew.

Wasn't that love?

She thought so.

The only love she wanted.

A couple of traitorous tears managed to escape from the corners of Haven's eyes, but Andino was quick to wipe them away before she could even acknowledge them. By the time the doctor came around to their room with the ominous manila folder already opened in his hand, Haven had resituated herself in her own chair.

She was still holding her husband's hand, though.

She needed that.

"Good news," the doctor said before he even looked up from the folder, "we have elevated HGC levels—positive for pregnancy. We're going to need to get you in for an ultrasound before you leave, Haven, because we want to see if it's a singleton, or if more embryos implanted. Congrats, guys. I know you were really hoping for this one."

Haven looked to Andino.

He was already staring at her with a smile.

One that was *knowing*.

Because, of course, he knew.

He always did.

One baby.

One single, tiny growing baby.

Their *boy*.

Those were the only thoughts racing through Haven's mind as Andino helped her down the three steps leading away from the clinic to where a waiting town car sat running on the curb. The driver in the front seat—not their usual man, Nate, but someone else she recognized—didn't even bother to get out because Andino stepped up to the back and opened the rear door.

He kept a hand on the door while Haven climbed into the back of the car. She was about to move over to let her husband inside the vehicle as well when she realized he hadn't actually moved at all.

"Aren't you coming?" she asked.

Andino gave her a rueful smile. "I'll follow behind later."

What?

"What are you—"

"Business," he replied simply. "I've been waiting for word on something. It came in while we were waiting inside for our results, but I didn't want to bring it up. Today was important, babe."

"Still is, Andi."

He nodded. "Yeah, but so is keeping you, the girls, and my little guy safe, hmm?"

The stress left her with a hard exhale. For a long while, the two of them stared at one another. Her, inside the car. Him, standing outside on the curb in his suit.

He always looked like he owned the city.

She supposed in a way, he did.

"Is it …" Haven let her words trail off, considering how she wanted to pose the question. "Is it about what happened a while back at the park?"

It wasn't like she had forgotten about that. Quite the opposite, really. The more time passed, well, it was never too far from her mind, really. Thing was, even if it pissed her off, she knew Andino would handle it. It's just what he did.

"It's just business, babe."

His mouth said one thing. His eyes said another.

Haven chose not to press for more. They all had to make those choices.

"Be safe. And come home."

Andino shrugged one shoulder. "It's the only place I want to go when the day is over, Haven."

Yeah. Her, too.

THIRTEEN

Andino watched the minute hand on his watch tick
past the twelve as he fixed the gold cufflink at his
wrist just because. He wasn't exactly the type to fidget
because he thought it was beneath him, honestly, but
there were times when it just could not be helped.
Now was one of those times.

His worst enemy was not actually his attitude or
asshole nature despite what others liked to say. In
fact, it was his boredom. He jokingly blamed that on
his parents and their insane need to feed into
whatever he'd wanted as a child—now that he was an
adult, he expected everyone around him to still do the
same they had. The worse the boredom became, the
quicker he was to simply leave a situation. Most times,
that wasn't a problem being who he was and all.

Not tonight, however.

At the moment, he had no choice but to wait in the dilapidated restaurant. Although after all these years, it no longer resembled what it once was. They certainly couldn't pass it off as a business under renovations when all someone needed to do was look at the crumbling walls to know better. Nonetheless, the business worked just fine for certain aspects of Andino's job, and since he was stuck with it—seeing as how it had been in the family longer than *he* had—it was as good as anywhere to murder someone.

Right?

A throat clearing across the room had Andino finally looking away from the watch on his wrist. He let go of the cufflink as well, resuming his previous position with his hands folded in his lap while he sat on the edge of what used to be a table. Or hell, maybe it had been a stationary counter. He couldn't be sure—there were no chairs to say either way and even the floor was just a mess of busted tiles that were no longer recognizable.

Across the space, one of two of his enforcers that he'd decided should stay inside the building with him glanced his way. Standing next to what used to be a window, but was now just a hole covered by slats of plywood, Nate nodded Andino's way.

Ah, good.

The show was just about ready to start.

He'd been waiting for his.

For too long, perhaps.

Well, if he were an honest man, he'd just say he'd been waiting for it since the man who had come all the way from New Zealand—only known and spoke about as Mr. Moshka—sent someone to deliver a message to Andino's wife. It was only made worse by the fact that his children had also been there that day.

Of course, nothing was ever easy.

Or simple.

Andino was also not a dumb man. He didn't rush into teaching someone a lesson without considering all possible avenues and what might or could come of it after it was all said and done. He needed plans *after* it was all over, too.

So, he waited.

Did his job.

And let others do theirs.

Now, it was finally coming together.

The quiet stillness of the rundown restaurant and the area outside allowed Andino the chance to hear his incoming guests be stopped by the men he had waiting at the doors that were also covered in plywood.

"Yes," one of his enforcers said, "you'll go in alone."

"That was not what I agreed—"

"Your boss either wants this meeting to happen, or he *doesn't.*"

Seconds ticked down.

Andino continued to wait.

Nothing more was said outside, however. In the next minute, the door was opened and a man dressed rather smartly in a three-piece, black on black suit stepped beyond the doorway. Andino recognized him on sight—before the man even spotted Andino across the room or his enforcers standing on either side of the door with guns already drawn and pointed at his temples—as the man who took Mr. Moshka's place at what should have been their first meeting months ago.

The one that Andino called off.

He wasn't surprised.

Mr. Moshka, human trafficker extraordinaire, had intended to use New York as his personal collection field for trafficking victims seeing as how the state was both a melting pot of different people *and* a sanctuary city. It was easy to overlook those who went missing when those people were either undocumented in the first place, or came from an already overlooked minority group.

He was not the first human trafficker to think he would be able to do business with Andino over the years, and he doubted the man would be the last. He was, however, one of the most irritating because he hadn't seemed to understand Andino wasn't interested.

Some people would sell their souls in that way.

He wasn't one of them.

It wasn't as though Andino was a saint—he didn't play the part, either. The entire Marcello empire had been built on the backs of people that would absolutely be considered victims. They made a great portion of their money in bribery, blackmail, illegal substance sales, a bit of smuggling between the States and Canada, and just a touch of arms dealing. They were criminals, absolutely.

They didn't touch skin.

He would not sell humans.

They never had.

Everybody had a line—this one was the Marcellos.

Andino hadn't intended to do business with Mr. Moshka—but he'd been willing to entertain the man's first meeting just so that he could tell him to stay the fuck out of the Marcello territory while doing his work.

But here they were.

And none of that happened.

It still wouldn't.

"Daniel Delwalsh, yes?" Andino asked from his perch.

The man's gaze finally focused through the darkness of the space and landed on Andino at the same time the guns pointed at either side of his head were racked and ready to fire. Outside the space, two muted *pops* echoed through the thin, crumbling walls. The following thumps were just morbid enough to tell Mr. Moshka's closest man—who also apparently handled most of his dealings with others, so he didn't have to be there firsthand—that the men who accompanied him were now dead on the ground.

"You'll soon follow," Andino said, voicing what he was sure were the man's inner thoughts and fears. *Good.* He wanted him afraid. "It'll be a well-earned message for your boss, who I am sure won't miss you all that much. He'll have you replaced before the week is out, won't he? Nonetheless, *my* message will be received as I intend for it to when I return you and your men outside to his doorstep—it took a while for me to find his address, you see."

"You're making a grave—"

Andino stepped down from the counter, his first move silencing the man instantly. "I don't make mistakes, actually. I have too much to lose in that case. Your unfortunate end won't be seen as an act of aggression against your boss considering the amount of times I've made it clear we wouldn't be doing business—this will simply settle it once and for all. I always do my research on the people who I see as threats, you understand? I know exactly who I am dealing with between you and your boss, and neither of you frighten me."

Each word he spoke brought him one step closer to the man caught between two enforcers and their guns. Not that they, or their weapons, would be needed.

Not when Andino had his own.

A foot away from Daniel, Andino pulled his own gun—his favorite, an Eagle—from beneath his suit jacket. He pulled back the safety, racked the weapon, and pulled the trigger as soon as it met the man's forehead. The spray of blood and matter was … unfortunate.

It stained his jacket.

That was fine.

"I have another blazer in the car, boss," Nate said quietly.

Andino stared at the dead man on the floor. "Good, appreciate that."

Nate nodded, but said nothing more.

"Make sure Mr. Moshka gets a call to his personal line to let him know what will soon be arriving to his doorstep—we wouldn't want it to be a surprise. Also let him know this concludes any possible business between the two of us, and should he try to come into my state again, he won't make it twenty-four hours before he meets the same fate."

"You got it, boss."

Andino sighed and tucked his warm gun away. "I'm ready to go home. I have a question to answer for my wife."

"Car's warm and ready whenever you are," Nate said.

"I'm ready, Nate."

He'd been ready for a while now.

FOURTEEN

Haven's life wasn't the same as it had once been in her early twenties—she could no longer afford to stay up until the wee hours of the morning and get up shortly after to start an entirely new day. She had kids, a *job*, and a whole house to take care of. She tried to be in bed and asleep by twelve, at the latest, unless it was a special occasion.

As the digital clock on the bedside table ticked beyond two A.M., with Haven still wide awake against her mound of pillows with the thought of sleep far from her mind. In fact, she thought about literally everything else *but* sleep even though that's what she needed to be doing the most.

So was the life of a mob boss's wife. She often wondered if Andino even realized how often his wife stayed awake at night worrying over things she had neither a say, nor any control over at the end of the day. Because she did it far more often than she wanted to admit.

With the house quiet and dark, Haven settled herself on staying awake until she heard that familiar rumble of an engine pulling into their garage. That was how she knew whatever *business* her husband had needed to handle that evening must have ended in some kind of bloodshed. He only used the garage when he didn't want a witness to see him enter the house. That way, there was always plausible deniability about who had come home late at night, and what they looked like when they exited the vehicle.

Or that's what he explained when she thought to ask once.

Sometimes, Haven wished she didn't ask.

It was easier.

It took a good ten minutes before her husband even darkened the doorway of their bedroom. She couldn't help but notice how the blazer he wore was a dark navy and not the flat black he'd worn with her earlier. She didn't mention it.

Nor did she say a thing about the spots of dried red *something* on the backs of his hands when he lifted one to wave her way. She pressed her lips together, but at the same time, couldn't stop the relieved smile that fettered over her lips at the sight of him.

"How'd things go?" she asked.

Yeah.

That was a safe way to ask.

Andino shrugged as he headed for the attached master bathroom. "It went well. I don't think there'll be anymore problems from that side of things, anyway."

A breath escaped her.

Then, another.

He had already disappeared into the bathroom, and she could hear the shuffle of clothing dropping to the floor. Without needing to be told, she knew those clothes would not be there come morning, and she wouldn't find them in his bag for dry cleaning, either. She wasn't sure if he burned them or simply threw the items away, but he never asked her to handle them.

She was grateful.

"Andino?"

"Hmm?"

Haven dragged in another lungful of air, feeling all that pressure in her chest that had been building up over the evening finally start to release. She hated that the very most. The weight that came with it, and the sensation it left behind even after it was already gone.

Those were things she couldn't forget.

She wished she could.

"What, babe?" he called from the bathroom.

The words wouldn't come out though she tried to make them. Everything stayed stuck in her mind and lungs like tar. She only wanted to tell him that she loved him—would *always* love him even when he did things she couldn't approve of or when their life scared her to fucking death. None of it mattered because at the end of the day, just like at the end of this one, she would still love him.

That was the choice *she* made.

Haven was fine with it.

Instead of trying to keep pretending like everything was fine—it mostly was, now—and trying to force the words out, Haven decided to try something different. Kicking the blankets from her legs, she slipped out of the bed, and headed for the bathroom.

She found Andino bent over the sink with bubbles of soap thick in his hands before he scrubbed them down his face with a few strokes of his palms. He quickly washed it away with the water spilling from the taps before turning it off and reaching for a towel he had waiting on the edge of the counter.

Haven didn't speak.

She didn't need to.

Andino glanced her way as though he knew she'd come to stand in the bathroom with him—maybe he'd heard her approach over the running water. Or maybe it was just because this man was entirely hers … heart *and* soul. Whether he was perfect or not didn't make a difference because he was perfect for *her*. He knew where she was. He felt her when she was nearby.

The way she did for him, too.

He turned away from the sink at the same time she moved toward him. His arms caught her easier, wrapping tightly around her back and shoulders while hers tightened at his middle. She inhaled his scent, listened to the steady beat of his heart, and waited as they synced in stillness and breaths.

All was good again.

Right again.

"Do you remember," he asked with his lips pressed against the top of her head, "when you asked me how I do this—be that man, and this one, too? You asked me why, *how* … I didn't have an answer. I wanted to think about it."

"Of course," she whispered.

Andino's arms tightened in just the right way around her. "I'll never be anybody else—this is me until the day I die. And somehow, despite being who I am, I managed to find a woman that loves me, who has given me three children—with my next on the way—a *home*, and a life. I intend to keep these things, they're mine, and that means protecting it by

103

whatever means necessary. So, I am *that* man because being him lets me do what I need to."

Haven said nothing.

She couldn't.

Andino didn't seem to mind when he pressed a kiss to the crown of her head and murmured, "You do the same thing—just in different ways. I know sometimes you think you're misplaced beside me, but no one is a better fit to stand there. I promise."

Forever his queen.

Or so he liked to say.

"I'll do this forever," he told her.

Haven tipped her head back to look up and meet his gaze. "Me, too."

He smiled. So did she.

It's why she wasn't at all surprised when his next kiss that came down upon her lips quickly went from sensual and sweet to something far more wicked and hot. If they were going to hell for everything they had done and what they were, then they might as well go together.

It only seemed fair.

Andino reminded Haven of every reason why and how he loved her when he lifted her to the bathroom counter, pulled the satiny sleep shorts down her legs to discard them on the floor, and fucked her against the large mirror of their vanity.

He was rough. His words, *dark*. Selfish.

He took so much from her.

Every single time.

She loved to give it to him, though.

Here they were, close to a decade into their marriage, and he still fucked her the same way he always had. *Wildly*. Like his soul was fighting to become one with hers. With an undercurrent of his ownership stamped in every kiss, touch, and stroke of his cock that filled her. Only he could do that to her.

Surrounded by their privilege, with his hands pinning her under his weight and love, she found that place where only Andino could take her to. Where the world didn't feel like the outside looking in, and nothing could ever touch them.

She loved him the most for that.

Always would.

FIFTEEN

Eight months later …

Giovanni Andino came early—only by a couple of
weeks, though. They expected it even though his
mother's entire pregnancy had been one of the easiest
out of all her children. They could see it coming with
every appointment where the boy seemed to measure
larger than he should be, and the doctors warned
everything pointed to an early baby.

Andino stared into the dark, hazy eyes of his
newborn son when he'd been placed on his mother's
chest right after he was born and found instantaneous
love. Each of his children had been a little different.
He found their connections in many ways.

With little G, it'd been the second he found his father.

That single *moment*.

They'd held off telling their daughters and the rest of their family they were pregnant until they had both had time to celebrate together privately. They did the same with announcing he would be a boy. Their family seemed to understand why they did things that way and never said anything about it.

Rather, everyone celebrated *with* them once they finally shared.

Like everything else about the pregnancy when they waited to share, Andino and Haven decided to wait to announce he was born until the next day—other than to his parents who came to grab the girls when he took Haven into the hospital.

G came home to meet his sisters first and his grandparents. It would be over the following days that the rest of the family trickled in to meet Andino's son. He liked it that way.

Andino certainly didn't want to share his son's time, but he forced himself to, anyway. Like today when his uncles came over to meet the baby. It was okay, though, because he knew that he still had the rest of his son's life to do and be everything he wanted for the boy.

He would be spoiled.

A proper *principe*.

As loved as his sisters. Andino's *only* son.

The last-born Marcello boy of his generation.

He realized, as he watched his newborn son from afar while his three uncles hovered over the baby's bassinet, their words too low for him to hear, that he had everything he'd ever wanted.

Andino hadn't realized what that meant until now.

He was a lucky fuck. Still an asshole, yes, but a lucky one. He would change nothing.

Interested in finding your next BK read? If you loved Andino and Haven's story, you might like the

Filthy Marcellos series, following the stories of Andino's grandfather, uncles, and even his father as they find their respective HEAs in the midst of trying to survive the world of mafioso.

Or maybe John's story, *John + Siena: The Complete Duet*, Andino's best friend and cousin dealing with his spiraling mental health fresh out of prison while a mafia war breaks out … all because he fell for the woman he wasn't supposed to have.

Happy reading!

XO,

BK.

BIO

Bethany-Kris is a Canadian author, lover of much, and mother to four young sons, three cats, and four dogs. A small town in Eastern Canada where she was born and raised is where she has always called home. With her boys under her feet, a snuggling cat, barking dogs, and a spouse calling over his shoulder, she is nearly always writing something ... when she can find the time.

Find all the places to stalk Bethany-Kris on her website at www.bethanykris.com.

OTHER BOOKS

The Guzzi Legacy

Corrado

Alessio

Chris

Beni

Bene

Marcus

Renzo + Lucia

Privilege

Harbor

Contempt

Andino + Haven

Duty

Vow

One Last Time

Andino + Haven: The Complete Duet

John + Siena

Loyalty

Disgrace

John + Siena: Extended

John + Siena: The Complete Duet

Cross + Catherine

Always

Revere

Unruly

The Companion

Naz & Roz

The Naz & Roz Chronicles

Guzzi Duet

Unraveled, Book One

Entangled, Book Two

DeLuca Duet

Waste of Worth: Part One

Worth of Waste: Part Two

Standalone Titles

Pretty Lies

Dirty Pool

Effortless

Inflict (**permanently free**)

Cozen

Captivated

Dishonored

Donati Bloodlines

Thin Lies

Thin Lines

Thin Lives

Behind the Bloodlines

The Complete Trilogy

Filthy Marcellos

Antony

Lucian

Giovanni

Dante

Legacy

A Very Marcello Christmas

The Complete Collection

Seasons of Betrayal

Where the Sun Hides

Where the Snow Falls

Where the Wind Whispers

Seasons: The Complete Seasons of Betrayal Series

Gun Moll Trilogy

Gun Moll

Gangster Moll

Madame Moll

The Chicago War

Deathless & Divided

Reckless & Ruined

Scarless & Sacred

Breathless & Bloodstained

The Complete Series

Maldives & Mistletoe

The Russian Guns

The Russian Guns

The Arrangement

The Life

The Score

Demyan & Ana

Shattered

The Jersey Vignettes

Fantasy Romance

The Hunted

Find more on Bethany-Kris's website at
www.bethanykris.com.